Pet Corner

FURRY HAMSTERS

By Katie Kawa

Gareth Stevens
Publishing

Please visit our website, www.garethstevens.com. For a free color catalog of all our high-quality books, call toll free 1-800-542-2595 or fax 1-877-542-2596.

Library of Congress Cataloging-in-Publication Data

Kawa, Katie.
Furry hamsters / Katie Kawa.
   p. cm. — (Pet corner)
ISBN 978-1-4339-5605-8 (pbk.)
ISBN 978-1-4339-5606-5 (6-pack)
ISBN 978-1-4339-5603-4 (library binding)
1. Hamsters as pets—Juvenile literature. I. Title.
SF459.H3K39 2011
636.935'6—dc22

                                        2010053826

First Edition

Published in 2012 by
Gareth Stevens Publishing
111 East 14th Street, Suite 349
New York, NY 10003

Copyright © 2012 Gareth Stevens Publishing

Editor: Katie Kawa
Designer: Andrea Davison-Bartolotta

Photo credits: Cover, pp. 1, 5, 7, 15, 17, 21, 23, 24 (paws, pouches) Shutterstock.com; pp. 9, 11, 13, 24 (pellets) iStockphoto.com; p. 19 iStockphoto/Thinkstock.

Printed in the United States of America

CPSIA compliance information: Batch #CS11GS: For further information contact Gareth Stevens, New York, New York at 1-800-542-2595.

Contents

Hamsters love to play!

A hamster runs to stay healthy. It runs in a wheel.

Hamsters run inside balls. This keeps them from getting lost.

A hamster lives in a cage. The cage is cleaned every week.

Hamsters eat special food. These are called pellets.

Hamsters eat fruits and vegetables too.

Hamsters have pouches in their cheeks. This is where they keep food.

A hamster chews its toys. This keeps its teeth short.

A hamster cleans itself.
It licks its paws and
wipes its fur.

Hamsters have soft fur. They like when people pet them.

Words to Know

paws

pellets

pouches

Index